THE REALLY REALLY LONG CHRISTMAS LIST

A Story by Carl Smith

Illustrations by Matt Whittaker

ISBN: 9781694808769

This book is dedicated to my children. Their childhood enthusiasm, joy, and hopeful innocence inspired this story. I am forever grateful for the gift of my children.

The boy in the red shirt was shocked when he heard what she had done. He couldn't believe what the other children were saying, and his voice quivered when he asked his friends "Is that her?"

The girl with the red ribbon in her hair answered, "Yes, that's her! Why would she do that? I don't understand!"

"I don't know what she was thinking either," whispered the blond haired girl, "but this is what I was told."

I heard that she was a little girl who always loved winter. That she loved to feel the cold crisp wind on her face. She loved to hear the sound of the icy snow popping and crackling under her warm winter boots, as she walked down the snow-covered lane to her house. She loved to watch the snowflakes floating through the air and she would run laughing and giggling as she tried to catch them on her tongue. She really loved winter.

But, most of all she loved winter,
because when winter was here

CHRISTMAS WAS NEAR!

She knew that this Christmas would be a really special one. She had been adding to her Christmas list all year long. Every day she would put new things on her list. Anything she could think of, toys, video games, sport equipment, clothing, and anything else that might be fun. Nothing took her away from her list. Even when her friends would knock on her door and ask her to come out and sled ride or build a snowman, she wouldn't leave her list. She could hear her friends laughing and playing outside, but she just had to keep writing.

AIL

Every day she would hurry home from school, do her homework, eat quickly and run to her room. She didn’t want to forget anything that she had thought of while she was at school. Sometimes when she skipped dessert, her mother would bring cookies up to her room for her. Often, she had to lay her pencil down, because her hand was so tired from writing. By winter's end, she had 523 gifts on her list.

Dear
Santa

In the spring when her sisters were swinging on the swing set, she kept writing. She could smell the flowers and hear the bees buzzing outside her window. She could hear the robins singing and the frogs croaking from the nearby pond. She could hear the other children laughing and playing, but she only listened for a minute. She just had to keep adding to her list.

Dear
Santa

In the summer, when her family would go on vacation, the little girl would take her list with her. Even at the beach, she would add to her list. She didn't dare go into the ocean. She sat under her umbrella, far from the water, because she didn't want her list to get wet. After all, Santa wouldn't be able to read a smeared and water soaked list. She was very careful.

Dear
Santa

In the fall, she would walk through the fallen, colored leaves, kicking them as she went. She would try to catch the leaves as they drifted and darted down through the cool, crisp fall air.
On Halloween, her second favorite holiday, she tried on her costume and was tempted to go trick-or-treating. She was ready to walk out the front door, but just then more gift ideas popped into her head. She didn't want to forget them, so she ran upstairs and added the new gifts to her list. When she started writing she couldn't stop. The ideas kept coming. She was on idea number 12,190 when she fell asleep. She was still wearing her witch's costume.

Finally, Christmas Eve arrived. She was so excited! She hurried and carried her really, really long Christmas list downstairs. She made 414 trips up and down the steps. She was so tired she had to stop in the middle of her work to rest.

When her parents saw the little girl's list they were really surprised. They told the little girl that she had better get to bed, because Santa was coming soon. The little girl ran up to her bed and tried to fall asleep, but even as she lay there, she thought of more things to put on the list. She knew she couldn't go back downstairs, because Santa might catch her awake and that would ruin everything. She was so excited.

Just as she was falling asleep, she thought she heard sleigh bells. Somebody was walking across her roof. Was it Santa? She pulled the covers up over her head and fell asleep.

Santa was very surprised by the little girl's list!
It was only two inches shorter than her Christmas tree.

With a puzzled grin and a nod of his head, Santa read the list. He called to his helper elves and began to unload the sleigh. Santa started with the first thing on the list and began to place the gifts under the tree. Santa stacked the gifts one sleigh load at a time.

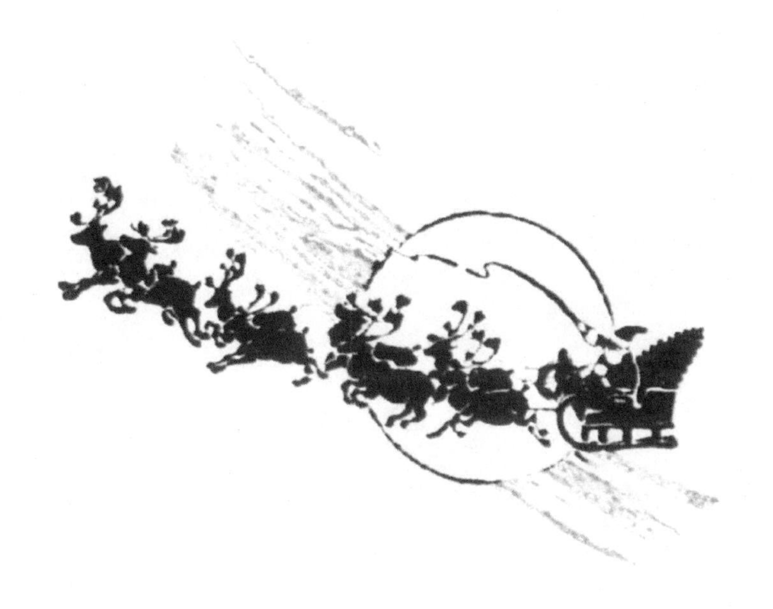

After each sleigh load, Santa had to go back to the North Pole to get even more presents. He piled gifts until they were stacked to the ceiling and covered the tree. The gifts filled the living room, the hall way, and spilled out the front door. Santa, his helper elves, and the reindeer were all getting very tired.

Many times that night, Santa flew back and forth to the North Pole. He tried very hard to make the little girl happy.

During the night the little girl was awakened by the sound of crackling snow on the roof. She heard reindeer running and the sound of tinkling sleigh bells. She jumped out of bed and ran to the window and saw Santa and his sleigh flying away from her house. On the ground, below her window, she saw presents for as far as she could see. The gifts were on the sidewalk and filled up the yard and went around the bend. Beautifully wrapped gifts with flowing ribbons decorated the entire countryside.

The winter rabbits stood on their hind legs trying to look over the boxes. The ducks couldn't get back to their pond, because the gifts blocked their way. The squirrels scuttered and scurried back and forth. They were very hungry and couldn't find the nuts that they had stored for the winter. Their winter food was buried somewhere under all those boxes.

The little girl ran down the stairs to get to her list. She turned the corner and slid to a stop. She couldn't go any further. There was a wall of gifts blocking her way.

She just had to get through. She began to climb up the huge mountain of gifts. As she got higher, the boxes began to wiggle, wobble, shimmy and shake. She held on tightly and was more than a little scared. To be safe, she lay down on top of the boxes and began to crawl over towards her really, really long Christmas list. She had to be careful not to bump her head on the ceiling fan. She inched her way across the tower of gifts and finally reached her list.

She looked at her list. Santa had circled the last three gifts on her list. Santa had written beside each of those gifts, “back at the North Pole”. She knew that Santa had to go back and get those gifts. He wasn’t done. She knew he was coming back.

She began to wonder where the things she really wanted were. She gasped, “They must be on the bottom! They were the very first things on my list!!”

Quickly she wrote Santa a note.

THE NOTE

Dear Santa,
The things that I really want are at the bottom of all these gifts, and I know it will take me months to unwrap all these presents and find those gifts. But, if I stop to eat, watch TV, read, or play video games, it will take years. Santa, I hope you understand that this year I want to build a snowman with my friends and swing on the swing set and jump in the water and get wet and I really want to go trick-or-treating. So Santa, please take all these gifts back and just leave the things I truly want.

Thank you Santa,
Me

She put the note on top of her list and crawled back over the gifts. She was very careful not to bump her head on the ceiling fan. She carefully climbed down the wiggly, wobbly pile of gifts and ran back upstairs to bed.

Santa came back with the last three gifts and found the note. Santa smiled and got to work. He tried very hard to make the little girl happy. Santa and his helper elves loaded sleigh after sleigh with the gifts. Santa flew all over the world that night giving the extra gifts to the children who weren't expecting any presents that year.

When the littlc girl woke up, she jumped from her bed and ran to her window. She was very excited. She could see her sidewalk and the countryside. Everything was covered in beautiful, fluffy white snow. She could see the rabbits hopping excitedly across the field. The ducks were swimming in the pond and the hungry squirrels were happily eating their acorns. All the gifts were gone.

She ran down the stairs and down the open hallway. She peeked into the living room and under her tree were just the presents she really wanted.

She was so happy!!!

Santa had taken all those gifts back!!!

Carl Smith is the father of seven children and grandfather of 17. His seven children inspired this humorous and relatable Christmas story. He is a lifelong resident of Western Pennsylvania and has been a special education teacher at a Pennsylvania county prison for 25 years. Carl is a published author in the correctional-education field. He has various writing projects currently in the works.

Made in the USA
Middletown, DE
23 December 2021

56940666R00022